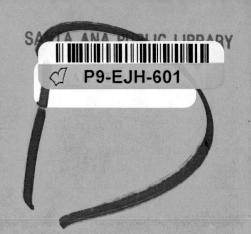

The THREE GOLDEN ORANGES

Retold by ALMA FLOR ADA

Illustrated by REG CARTWRIGHT

ATHENEUM BOOKS *for* YOUNG READERS

Atheneum Books for Young Readers
An imprint of Simon & Schuster Children's Publishing Division
1230 Avenue of the Americas
New York, New York 10020

Book design by Michael Nelson

The text of this book is set in Post Medieval.
The illustrations are rendered in oil paint.

Printed in Hong Kong
First Edition
10 9 8 7 6 5 4 3 2 1

Library of Congress Cataloging-in-Publication Data:
Ada, Alma Flor.
The three golden oranges / retold by Alma Flor Ada ; illustrated by Reg Cartwright.
p.   cm.
Summary: Acting on the advice of the old woman on the cliff by the sea, three
brothers who wish to find brides go in search of three golden oranges.
ISBN 0-689-80775-9
[1. Fairy tales. 2. Folklore–Spain.] I. Cartwright, Reg, ill. II. Title.
PZ8.A2137Th   1999
398.2–dc21   [E]
97-47570

To my grandaughters, Jessica Emily, Cristina Isabel, and Victoria Ann,
three sources of light and joy. May you always be best friends
with one another.
—A. F. A.

For Hugh
—R. C.

T HE SETTING SUN CAST A GOLDEN GLOW upon the
simple whitewashed house as three brothers–
Santiago, Tomás, and Matías–returned home from
the fields. The older two walked briskly ahead,
unburdened, while behind them followed their
younger brother, Matías, shouldering sheaves of
wheat as sweat dripped from his brow.

"Sit down and rest a while," said Sara, their mother.
"I would like to speak to the three of you."

When the young men sat down, she announced:
"I am ready to be a grandmother. I have decided that
the time has come for you to find wives and start
your own families. So I suggest you begin courting
the women of your choice at once."

The three brothers looked at each other worriedly.
They knew there were no unmarried women in the
entire valley that stretched from the mountains to the
sea. When they returned to the fields the next day,
they couldn't stop wondering about this problem.

"WHY DON'T WE ASK THE OLD WOMAN who lives on the cliff by the sea?" suggested Matías. His brothers agreed, much to Matías's surprise, since they rarely paid attention to him.

The three climbed up the narrow path to the high cliff overlooking the ocean. The old woman was spinning wool in front of the cave that was her home.

"What brings you here?" she asked without stopping her work.

"We'd like to get married, and we have come to ask your advice," explained Matías simply and courteously.

"And what kind of wives do you want?" asked the old woman.

"I want a wife who is very beautiful," Santiago said immediately.

"I want a wife who is very rich and beautiful," added Tomás without a pause.

"And you?" asked the old woman, seeing that Matías had remained silent.

"I'd like to find a young woman who is kind, joyful, and someone I could love very much," answered Matías.

"Each of you can obtain what you want. But in order to find your wives, you will need to work together. For three days you will walk toward that mountain," she said, pointing to a barren slope whose peak lay hidden among the clouds. "On the other side of the mountain, there is a castle surrounded by an orange grove. All the oranges will still be green. But in one tree, you will find three golden oranges on a single branch. Pick all three of the oranges without hurting the branch. Bring them to me, and you will have the wives that you desire. But remember this: Woe to you if you do not follow my advice!"

THE YOUNG MEN QUICKLY RETURNED HOME to prepare for their journey. The next day, after filling their pockets with nuts, dates, and bread, they set forth.

All day they walked. When night fell, they settled in a barn and went to sleep in a haystack. But a while later, Santiago was awakened by a moonbeam that shone through the door of the barn. "Why am I wasting time here with my two brothers?" he asked himself. "When we find the oranges, we'll probably end up fighting over the best one. If I get there first, I'll choose the one I like best, and my brothers can fight over the other two."

And so, Santiago got up and walked the rest of the night and all the following day. Early on the morning of the third day, he arrived at the castle.

THE SUN'S RAYS had barely begun to warm the
orange grove. The white orange blossoms shone
in the morning light, and indeed, all of the oranges
were still green.

Just as Santiago despaired of ever finding the
golden oranges, he was drawn by the glow of a tree
next to the castle doors. On the tree's highest branch
shone three oranges, as bright as the purest gold.

The branch was too high to reach, but Santiago
was not about to give up now. He grasped the tree
to see if he could shake the oranges loose. Much
to his surprise, he found that his hand stuck to the
trunk of the tree. He was trapped.

Right then an old man came out of the castle,
accompanied by several guards. With a tap of his
magic wand, the old man freed Santiago, who was
then promptly captured by the guards and thrown
into a dungeon.

From his dark cell, Santiago heard the old man
crying to himself: "Oh my good wife, my precious
daughters. How long will you be imprisoned?"

WHEN TOMÁS AND MATÍAS WOKE UP and saw that Santiago had betrayed them, they quickly set out. At sundown, they found a cave on the side of the mountain where they could spend the night. As soon as Matías was asleep, Tomás rose quietly. "Santiago has gone ahead, but I'll catch up to him," Tomás thought. "I'll leave foolish Matías behind to manage as best he can."

It was midmorning of the third day when Tomás saw the castle. Santiago was nowhere in sight. Tomás marveled at the smell of the orange blossoms. He saw that all of the oranges were green, and then found himself irresistibly drawn to the light that shone from the tree by the castle doors.

When he saw the golden oranges, he threw himself at the tree in a frenzy, only to find his entire body stuck, unable to move. A few moments later, the old man tapped him with his wand, and the guards carried him to the same dungeon where his brother lay.

This time, both of them heard the old man's laments: "Oh my poor wife, my precious daughters, imprisoned by a terrible wizard . . ."

WHEN MATÍAS WOKE UP he was very sad to see that Tomás had also abandoned him. "I should hurry," he said to himself. "The old woman by the sea told us to stay together." Still, it was the afternoon of the third day by the time Matías reached the castle. Enraptured by the sweet fragrance of the orange blossoms, he allowed the scent to guide him, and soon found himself in front of the tree with the three golden oranges.

"I must pick the oranges quickly and go find my brothers," said Matías to himself. He jumped up and grabbed the branch on which the oranges grew. As the branch broke, the tree let forth a cry, and instantly the old man and the guards appeared before him.

"You already have the oranges so I cannot imprison you," said the old man.

"Where are my brothers, please?" asked Matías.

"The oranges will open all doors," said the old man. "Take nothing more than bread and water, and do not harm the oranges, or the same doors will close again."

Matías ran to the castle, where indeed the heavy doors swung open before him. Inside, the tall walls of the castle were covered with magnificent tapestries. Matías felt especially drawn to one that showed a young woman in a valley filled with orange groves. Reluctantly, he tore himself away to continue his search for his brothers.

When at last he found them, the dungeon's door swung open easily.

"Please forgive us for abandoning you," Santiago and Tomás pleaded.

"That does not matter now," answered Matías. "We must take the oranges to the old woman by the sea."

SANTIAGO AND TOMÁS, lured by the splendors that filled the castle, followed Matías unwillingly. "We must not touch anything," warned Matías. "Take only some bread and water for the journey." But as they followed Matías out of the castle, his older brothers secretly stuffed their pockets with whatever gold and silver objects were within reach.

Matías walked quickly, without stopping to eat or drink. Even though the sun was very hot, the oranges remained fresh and luxuriant.

But before they had gotten very far from the castle, his two older brothers had already eaten all their bread and drunk their water, without a thought for the next two days.

That night, the brothers decided to stay in an abandoned shepherd's hut. But Santiago could not sleep. He was angry that his youngest brother was carrying the oranges, and that he, the eldest, had failed at the task. So at midnight, he got up and took the largest orange from the branch that his sleeping brother held. Then he continued on alone.

SANTIAGO WALKED THE REST OF THAT NIGHT and all the next morning. Soon he was overwhelmed by the heat of the sun and felt he would die of thirst. At last, when he could stand it no longer, he decided to eat the juicy orange. But when he split it in half, there appeared in front of him a beautiful young woman.

"Please give me some bread," asked the woman.

"I don't have any. I ate it all," was all Santiago could say.

"Give me some water, then," she requested.

"I drank it all," he answered hopelessly.

"Then I must return to my orange and my tree," said the young maiden. After she disappeared, Santiago found himself swept up in a whirlwind of dust. Suddenly the castle walls rose before him again. He was dazed and confused as the guards captured him and returned him to the dungeon.

Meanwhile, Tomás woke up at dawn. When he saw that Santiago had disappeared with one of the oranges, he decided to follow his older brother's example. He took the larger of the two remaining oranges and went on his way, leaving Matías sleeping peacefully.

Tomás also found the rocky path and the burning sun unbearable, and decided that it would be better to eat the orange than to die of thirst. When he began to peel the orange, he, too, was surprised to see suddenly before him the most beautiful young woman that he ever could have imagined. And from the precious jewels that adorned her clothing, he could tell that she was indeed very rich.

"Please give me some bread," she asked.

"I don't have any. I ate it all," was all Tomás could say.

"May I have some water, then," she requested.

"I drank it all," he said unhappily.

"Then I must return to my orange and my tree," said the maiden. When she disappeared, Tomás found himself swept away in a whirlwind of dust and transported to the walls of the castle. In an instant, the guards took him prisoner and threw him in the dungeon with Santiago.

WHEN MATÍAS WOKE UP and saw that there was only one orange left, he felt very sad for his brothers. "How impatient they are!" he thought. With the bread and water he had saved, Matías was able to traverse the hot, dry valley. By evening, he had reached the sea and the old woman's cave.

"I see that you have broken the branch and separated the three oranges," said the old woman. "Because you have not followed my instructions, I will not be able to spare any of you from the misfortune that will result." Then the old woman cut the orange in half, and out flew a white dove.

"What about my bride?" asked Matías. "And what about my brothers?"

"All is not over yet," said the old woman. "Return to your home and to your fields, and wait. And continue always to follow your heart."

With no further words, she went back into her cave.

MATÍAS RETURNED HOME SADLY to tell his mother of their adventures and misfortunes. Although Sara was saddened by the disappearance of her older sons, she was very happy to have Matías back.

And every morning, after Matías went out to the fields, Sara was comforted by a white dove that came to rest on her shoulder. The dove kept her company all day while she did her chores. Somehow, Sara found herself trusting that everything would turn out all right.

ONE MORNING, when summer was almost over, Matías abandoned the fields and returned home early. "I've decided to return to the castle to see if I can find my brothers," he announced to his mother. Then his gaze fixed upon the white dove that was perched on her shoulder.

"Mother, where did that dove come from?" he asked.

"She comes to me every day to keep me company while you are in the fields," answered Sara. "I call her Blanquita."

Matías extended his hand and the dove perched upon it. As he stroked her gently, Matías found a thorn that was buried in the dove's neck, and he carefully removed it. Instantly, the dove turned into a young woman.

"My name is Blancaflor," she said. "Let us go quickly, there is no time to lose. I will accompany you to the castle."

Tʜɪs ᴛɪᴍᴇ, ᴛʜᴇ ᴊᴏᴜʀɴᴇʏ sᴇᴇᴍᴇᴅ sʜᴏʀᴛ. As they traveled, Blancaflor told Matías how her sisters, her mother, and she herself had all been cursed by a wicked sorcerer when her father refused to force any of his daughters to marry him.

"It is a woman's right to choose whom she wants to marry, don't you think?" she said. Matías wondered what he could do to persuade her to choose him.

When they reached the orange grove, all of the oranges were now ripe. But Blancaflor led Matías directly to the tree from which he had torn the branch. There hung the other two golden oranges.

Matías lifted Blancaflor so that she could reach the branch, and she carefully picked the two oranges. As soon as she placed them on the grass, they turned into her two sisters. Instantly the old man emerged from the castle, overtaken by joy. The tree shook and quivered, and then, right before everyone's eyes, it too turned into a woman.

"Mother!" cried the three young women. Their father embraced his wife and kissed each of his daughters on both cheeks.

"Meet my mother and my father," Blancaflor said to Matías. "And my sisters, Zenaida and Zoraida."

"Now I must find my brothers," Matías told Blancaflor.

"All of the doors are now open," said the old man, pointing to the castle door, where Santiago and Tomás had appeared.

Matías and Blancaflor both greeted the brothers, but when Santiago asked Zenaida if she would marry him, she answered: "I'd rather live alone than with a foolish vain man."

And when Tomás asked Zoraida if she would marry him, she answered: "I'd rather live alone than with a foolish greedy man."

So there was only one wedding in the castle. And after that, Matías and Blancaflor returned to the little white house next to the sea, where they filled the windowsills with potted geraniums and Sara's heart with joy.

No one really knows what happened to Santiago and Tomás, but if I ever find out I will be happy to tell you.

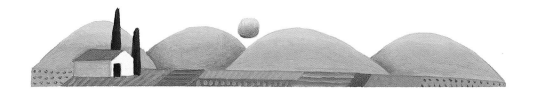

As we say in Spanish,

Colorin colorado
este cuento se ha acabado
This story entered by a silver path
and exited through a gold road
and I hope you liked it as much as I did
when my grandmother told it to me.

AUTHOR'S NOTE

The popular story of Blancaflor, the youngest of three sisters who is bewitched and held prisoner inside an orange, has taken many forms over time.

In some of the versions of the Blancaflor story she is actually held prisoner by her own father for defying him. A common element in many of the various versions is her transformation into a dove and the presence of a straight pin, stuck in her hand, that is the key to undoing the enchantment. The latter, of course, appears in my adaptation in Matías's act of removing the thorn from the neck of the dove. However, Blancaflor's father is clearly not her captor so much as a victim, of sorts, of the enchantment too.

Oranges were brought into Spain by the Arabs who held kingdoms in southern Spain from 711 to 1492. Orange trees are a favorite in the gardens of this region since they offer both flowers of exquisite fragrance and delicious fruit. The region of Valencia is especially famous for its orange groves, and oranges constitute one of its biggest exports.

—A. F. A.